E. B. Crisman

A Scriptural Argument

Infant baptism in a nut-shell

E. B. Crisman

A Scriptural Argument
Infant baptism in a nut-shell

ISBN/EAN: 9783337392703

Printed in Europe, USA, Canada, Australia, Japan

Cover: Foto ©Andreas Hilbeck / pixelio.de

More available books at **www.hansebooks.com**

A

SCRIPTURAL ARGUMENT.

INFANT BAPTISM

IN A NUT-SHELL.

BY E. B. CRISMAN, D. D.

THIRD EDITION; REVISED AND ENLARGED.

ST. LOUIS, MO.:

PERRIN & SMITH, BOOK AND JOB PRINTERS, 210 OLIVE STREET.

1880.

CONTENT S.

CHAPTER I.

Covenant Relation of Infants to the Church.

CHAPTER II.

New Testament Argument.

CHAPTER III.

Testimony of the Fathers.

CHAPTER IV.

Some Other Arguments.

CHAPTER V.

Some Objections Answered.

CHAPTER VI.

The Argument Condensed.

INFANT BAPTISM.

CHAPTER I.

COVENANT RELATION OF INFANTS TO THE CHURCH.

THE subject of the relation of the children of Christian parents to the Church, and of their rights as secured by that relation, is one which has perplexed many good people. The differences of views on this subject have caused unfortunate strifes, which bring the cause of our common Christianity into more or less disrepute with the outside world.

In entering upon the discussion of this subject, I make the following remarks:

1. I neither desire nor expect to con-

vince an opponent by abusing or ridiculing his views. A timid man may be moved by ridicule, and a resentful one by abuse, but an intelligent one will never be convinced by either.

2. God has made men with as great variety of minds as he has of features, and it must not be expected that all men will think alike on any subject.

3. The great subject of the salvation of sinners is of such absorbing importance that it would seem that it alone should occupy the attention of the Christian minister. But the apostolic injunction is, to be ready to give a reason for the faith which is in us, and self-defense is the first great law of nature. Therefore, we are ready and willing to set forth plainly the reasons for our views and practices, always observing that dignified and Heaven-approved charity, which embraces all the lovers of our Lord Jesus Christ.

The occasional necessity for this course will appear from the following incident in my own history: In the year 1857, at a camp-meeting in Western Texas, I was requested to preach on the subject of Infant Baptism, and did so on Saturday afternoon, and on the next day when an opportunity was given a number of parents came forward and dedicated their children to God—one presenting as many as five children, and another four, showing that they had previously neglected this duty. One of these parents informed me that he had been a member of the Cumberland Presbyterian Church for twelve years, and while he had in that time repeatedly heard the practice of Infant Baptism abused and ridiculed, he had never before heard any man defend it, and had consequently neglected it in his own family up to that time.

After the above introduction, I proceed

to consider the following proposition:

THAT THE CHILDREN OF PARENTS WHO ARE MEMBERS OF THE CHURCH HAVE ALWAYS HELD SUCH COVENANT RELATION TO THE CHURCH AS ENTITLED THEM TO RECEIVE THE ORDINANCE WHICH WAS AND IS A SEAL OF THAT COVENANT.

In arguing this proposition I will mention:

1. That the Church under the New Testament dispensation and the Church under the Old Testament dispensation are not separate organizations, but are identical—one Church. Not one Church for the old dispensation, which was done away with, and another Church established for the new dispensation, as some do erroneously argue; but one body, perpetual, never destroyed nor disorganized, extending from the earliest age of promise and covenant to the last work of grace on earth. Thus, it is that great building

erected "on the foundation of the apostles and prophets, Jesus Christ himself being the chief corner-stone in whom all the building fitly framed together groweth to an holy temple in the Lord." From this Scripture it is evident that it is not one building and foundation for the prophets or ancient times and another for the apostles or modern times; but one and the same building and foundation for both.

Also read the language of our Savior, Matthew xxi. 33–43, where the great and only change which took place in the Church, in passing from the old to the new dispensation, is forcibly represented by the parable of the vineyard which was let out to husbandmen who proved unfaithful, and the question is asked, What will the master do in the case? Would he destroy the vineyard and make a new one? By no means. But "he will miserably destroy those wicked men, and will let out his vineyard unto other husbandmen.'' Here the similitude is complete. The Church *at the first*, was ''let out'' to the Jews. They proved unfaithful and the Lord did not, therefore, destroy the Church and make a new one—but simply took it from the Jews and gave it to the Gentiles. ''The kingdom of God shall be taken from you'' (Jews) ''and given to a nation bringing forth the fruits thereof.'' Nothing can teach more plainly that the Church is continued from the old dispensation to the new. Not a new one built, but the old one more fully established and glorified. The same truth is also taught by our Savior, John x. 16.

In the epistle to the Romans the apostle Paul also bears testimony to the same truth under the similitude of the ''olive tree''— the natural branches of which—the Jews —were broken off because of unbelief, and the Gentiles, who ''were wild by nature, were grafted, contrary to nature, into a good olive tree." Not that the olive tree—the Church—was destroyed; that was preserved; but the Jews, to whom it was first given, were cast off, and the Gentiles grafted in—not made into a new or different Church, but put into *the very same* out of which the Jews had been cast.

Thus, according to Christ and St. Paul, *the Church is identically the same body now that it was in the days of old.* And he who is not convinced by such authority, "would not believe though one should rise from the dead."

2. That the Church has always had, and now has, two ordinances, typifying the two great and essential facts in the history of redemption, viz: the sufferings of Christ and the new birth. Without either one of these two facts no man is saved. Wherever both exist, the man is

saved whatever may be the other circumstances in special cases. Hence these are
the essential facts in redemption, and the
only essential facts. They are the two
facts symbolized by ordinances, and the
only facts thus symbolized and dignified.
No other facts can compare with them in
importance, and hence none are dignified
with them by representation in the ordinances. The object of the ordinances
has always been to keep these two essential facts prominently before the world.

In the Church at the present day, the
Lord's supper most forcibly typifies the
sufferings of Christ for human redemption, especially as seen in his broken body
and shed blood; and baptism, using the
purifying element, water, typifies the
washing of regeneration, the cleansing of
the soul from sin by the blood of Jesus
Christ, the new birth.

Of course, then, we cannot admit as

true, what our Baptist brethren claim, i. e. : that baptism represents the death, burial and resurrection of Christ. This we cannot admit for a number of reasons, the one here presented being itself a convincing one : We would by this view have both the ordinances of the Church representing Christ's sufferings and the other equally essential fact in redemption, the new birth, not represented at all in the ordinances. This argument is overwhelming when it is considered :

First. That, to secure redemption, which is the object of grace in all its provisions, the new birth is equally as essential as the atonement, and has equal claims to representation by ordinances.

Second. That one ordinance is enough to represent one thing, and hence that two to represent the same thing would be a work of superfluity in ordinances.

Third. That there can be no sufficient

reason assigned for typifying one of the two essential facts by two ordinances and leaving the other without a type.

What the Lord's supper and baptism accomplish now was done anciently by the passover and circumcision. The office performed in the two cases is identically the same. The sacrifices pointed forward by type to the same vicarious sacrifice back to which the mind is now directed by the solemn scene of the supper. The one assisted the prospective faith of the ancient, the other assists the retrospective faith of the modern Christian. What baptism now accomplishes by typifying the washing of regeneration, or the cleansing the soul from sin, was done by the sign of circumcision by typifying *that* "circumcision which is in the spirit, and not in the letter"—the circumcision of the heart being the washing of regeneration.

3. That I do not admit as true, what is usually understood by the expression, "Baptism has taken the place of circumcision." As though baptism is one ordinance and circumcision another.

Baptism, as an ordinance, has not taken the place of circumcision, as an ordinance. Circumcision and baptism are different forms of the same ordinance—the ordinance having identically the same signification and use under both forms. The ordinance of baptism of the new dispensation is,—not has taken the place of,—the ordinance of circumcision of the old dispensation. The circumcision of the old is,—not has given place to,—the baptism of the new. So likewise in signification and use the Lord's supper of the new is the passover of the old dispensation, and *vice versa*.

Justin Martyr, who had the personal instructions of those who had seen and heard the apostles to aid him in the interpretation of their writings, and the ancient fathers of the Church, called baptism "Christian Circumcision." We quote one sentence of Martyr, writing only forty years after the apostolic age: "We are circumcised by baptism—by Christ's circumcision." And one paragraph of Chrysostom, writing two hundred and eighty years after the apostolic age: "Our circumcision—I mean the grace of baptism—gives cure without pain, and has no determinate time as that had (the eighth day), but it is lawful to one at the beginning of life (first day of his birth), or in the middle of it, or in old age, to receive this circumcision, made without hands." He also enumerates the benefits of baptism, and adds, "For this cause we baptize infants also, that they be not defiled by sin."

Rev. Dr. John Guthrie, recently of

Glasgow, Scotland, whose very superior little book, "The Pædobaptist Guide," I have read since the previous edition of this work was issued, writes: "I understand baptism to be a sign of the purifying work of God the Spirit, just as the sister ordinance is a sign of the atoning work of God the Son. The other meanings imported into it by Baptists—grounded on their misinterpretation of the phrase, 'buried with Christ in baptism'—we utterly reject, as based on error, and as creating boundless confusion. BAPTISM IS A SIGN OF THE SPIRIT'S WORK, AS THE LORD'S SUPPER IS OF CHRIST'S WORK: here is a complete and symmetrical account of the two emblematical ordinances of Christianity, embracing between them the two most vital and central doctrines of redemption. That baptism does signify the outpoured influences of the Holy Spirit I need not stop to prove; for this Baptists admit (though they confuse it with other additions.) In reference to infants, no less than to adults, baptism is a sign of the Spirit's work, which is held by us to embrace, in its provision and scope, infants as well as adults, and to have special scope and significance in Christian households."

Thus the two ordinances which stood as types of the two great facts in the history and work of redemption, have never been changed—never abrogated—never displaced. Like the Church itself, they are *identically the same* now that they have always been. Like the Church, and for reasons which might be assigned, they have undergone changes in form,—*but in form only*,—in signification and use they are unchanged and unabrogated, being the same in unchangeable substance and type that they have ever been.

4. That, whatever God, originally es-

tablished as law and practice in the Church must continue to be law and practice until annulled by Him. Whoever denies the truth of this proposition is driven immediately into the bosom of the Roman Catholic Church, where the pope is held to be the vice-gerent of God and Christ in the government of the Church and may change its regulations at will.

It then remains for us to prove,

5. *That God in founding the Church originally enacted that the children of covenanting, or believing, parents should be admitted, in the church, to the same covenant relation as the parents enjoyed.*

For the first full and distinct development of a church organization we must refer to the time of Abraham. Him God separated from the heathen; with him entered into a covenant, appointing circumcision to be a sign and seal of that covenant. In this covenant he promised to be a God to him and to his seed forever.

Read Gen. xvii. 7: "And I will establish my covenant between me and thee and thy seed after thee in their generations, for an everlasting covenant, to be a God unto thee and to thy seed after thee."

Notice also in the above that the covenant then established was an everlasting covenant, not to end with a generation nor with a dispensation: as also in the following:

I. Chron. xvi. 15-17: "Be ye mindful always of his covenant; *the word which he commanded to a thousand generations*, even of the covenant which he made with Abraham, and of his oath unto Isaac; and hath confirmed the same to Jacob for a law, and to Israel for an everlasting covenant."

Here it is affirmed that the Abrahamic covenant is to continue for "a thousand generations," yea, forever. And of this covenant circumcision was the sign or token as seen in the following:

Gen. xvii. 11: "And ye shall circumcise the flesh of your foreskin; *and it shall* be a token of the covenant betwixt me and you."

And also a seal: Rom. iv. 11: "And he received the sign of circumcision, a seal of the righteousness of the faith which he had, yet being uncircumcised."

Circumcision being the sign or token of the covenant, of course all who were admitted to circumcision, were included in the covenant. Then we are ready to read the following: Gen. xvii. 12-13: "And he that is eight days old shall be circumcised among you, every man child in your generations, he that is born in the house, or bought with money of any stranger, which is not of thy seed. He that is born in thy house, and he that is bought with thy money, must needs be circumcised; and my covenant shall be in your flesh for an everlasting covenant."

And, Exod. xii. 43-44: "And the Lord said unto Moses and Aaron, this is the ordinance of the passover: There shall no stranger eat thereof: but every man's servant that is bought for money, when thou hast circumcised him, then shall he eat thereof." And verses 48 and 49: "And when a stranger shall sojourn with thee, and will keep the passover to the Lord, let all his males be circumcised, and then let him come near and keep it; and he shall be as one that is born in the land: for no uncircumcised person shall eat thereof. One law shall be to him that is home-born, and unto the stranger that sojourneth among you."

By carefully considering all the above quoted scriptures the following propositions will appear incontrovertible :

1st. That God in admitting the head of a household, whether Jew or Gentile, to the covenant, did not divide families by covenanting with the parents and leaving out the children.

2nd. That circumcision did not bring its subject into spiritual relation with God, but only into covenant relation, it being only an outward *sign* of the circumcision of the heart in the spirit. Rom. ii. 28, 29.

3d. The visible relation of the Jews to the visible Church was recognized by visible circumcision.

4th. It was made the imperative duty of the Jews in the visible Church to circumcise their male children at eight days old and upwards.

5th. It was allowed to a stranger—a

Gentile—to live among the Jews without circumcision.

6th. But if the Gentile should wish to enjoy the privileges of the visible Church he "must needs be circumcised."

7th. It was required of the Jews—or members of the Church—in admitting a Gentile, that they should not only require him to submit to circumcision himself, but that he should also circumcise "all his males."

And hence,

8th. *That in the original constitution of the Church, God ordained that every covenant relation, every covenant promise and every covenant requirement should apply to and include the infants as fully as the parents.*

We are now ready for remark,

6. That this covenant relation, which secures the title of infants to the visible ordinance which is its sign and seal, must

endure as long as the covenant itself shall endure. The durability of the covenant wherever mentioned, is declared to be "everlasting." Only one limit is given for the continuance of the relation between God and believing parents and their children, namely, a "thousand generations," which, doubtless, is an expression to denote its endless perpetuity; but if taken literally, it secures the title of infants to the sealing ordinance for a period of at least thirty thousand years, less than one-fifth of which has as yet transpired.

7. That these appointments and requirements of what Stephen called in New Testament times, "the Church in the wilderness," to which Moses belonged, were never annulled and can never be changed:

1st. *The law did not annul them:* Gal. iii. 17: "And this I say, that the covenant, that was confirmed before of

God in Christ, the law, which was four hundred and thirty years after"—at Mount Sinai—"cannot disannul, that it should make the promise of none effect."

2nd. *The Gospel did not annul them:* But rather confirmed them: Acts ii. 39: "For the promise is unto you, and to your children." Acts. iii. 25: "Ye are the children of the prophets, and of the cove- nant which God made with our fathers." Mark x. 14: "Suffer the little children to come unto me, and forbid them not: for of such is the kingdom of God." The "kingdom of God"—in Matthew the "kingdom of heaven"—meaning here, as often elsewhere, the Church.

Here we quote the learned and perti- nent remarks of Dean Alford in his "Greek Testament." In considering the last quoted and the succeeding verse of Scripture, he says: "We can hardly read our Lord's solemn saying, without seeing that it reaches further than the mere then present occasion. It might one day become a question whether the new Christian covenant of repentance and faith could take in the unconscious infant, as the old covenant did :—whether when Jesus was no longer on earth, little children might be brought to him, dedicated to his service, and made partakers of his blessing? Nay, in the pride of the human intellect, this question was sure one day to be raised; and our Lord furnishes the Church, by anticipation, with an answer to it for all ages. Not only may the little infants be brought to him, but in order for us, who are mature, to come to him, we must cast away all that wherein our maturity has caused us to differ from them, and BECOME LIKE THEM. Not only is infant baptism *justified*, but it is THE NORMAL PATTERN OF ALL BAPTISM : none can enter God's kingdom except *as an infant*.

In adult baptism, the *exceptional case*, we strive to secure that state of simplicity and childlikeness, which in the infant we have ready and undoubted to our hands."

3rd. God himself would not change the covenant. Once established it partakes of the nature of a contract, which is necessarily perpetual until both parties agree to cancel or change it. God having made the covenant between himself and the Church, guaranteeing certain privileges and blessings to themselves and to their children, as previously shown, that covenant must remain perpetual until such time as both parties agree to annul it.

In conclusion :

1st. Circumcision was both in the letter and spirit; i. e. : there was a literal circumcision and a spiritual circumcision. The same ordinance, in its changed form, baptism, is also both in the letter and spirit, i. e.: water baptism and the baptism of the Holy Ghost. This literal ordinance, both under its ancient and modern forms, serves a threefold purpose in the Church: 1st. It typifies the inward grace of spiritual cleansing. 2nd. It seals the admission to the covenant relation in the Church. 3rd. It binds its subjects to an observance of the whole law—Gal. v. 3. Whoever is once put in possession of the title to this sealing ordinance by the proper authority, enjoys a perpetual right to it. God adopted the infants of covenanting parents into the covenant relation, and gave them title to the sealing ordinance, and their claim to it is therefore perpetual.

2nd. When God has made it the duty of parents to seal their children in this covenant relation with him, they may not decline or neglect unless they can show that God has released them from the per-

30 INFANT BAPTISM.

formance. God has never changed his
appointments on this subject. It is therefore the imperative duty of all Christian
parents to dedicate their children to God
in the sealing ordinance of his own ap-
pointment.

3d. If the views set forth in this argument are not correct, and infant membership is not to be recognized, then I
will ask any opponent to show where and
when Christ became a member of the
Church? If the views of our opponents
on this subject be correct, then Christ
must have lived and died out of the
Church.

4th. The views and practice of Anti-
pædo-Baptists on this important subject
are unnatural and opposed to all ordinary
analogies. When a shepherd gathers his
flocks into the fold to protect them from
ravenous wolves, he does not gather in
the grown sheep and leave the lambs

without. Why should the great spiritual Shepherd pursue a different course in gathering his spiritual sheep into the spiritual fold? When the herdsman turns out his cattle in Spring and Summer to graze upon the hill sides and valleys, he is careful that the young shall first be marked and branded with the same marks and brands as the parent cattle bear. But our Baptist brethren would have us be less careful of our children in spiritual things, than we are of our lambs, pigs and calves in natural things.

We quote the following from a private letter recently received from a friend: "Parents are accountable for their children until a certain age. This imposes a fearful responsibility upon them. They must have every spiritual and ecclesiastical advantage in order to meet this responsibility. To do so the child ought to be in the Church with them—*where they*

are—not somewhere else. Admit the
parent, shut the door against the child,
and place a partition wall between them—
shut the ewe up in the sheep-fold and
place the lamb outside and can she suckle
it?''

The sign and seal of the covenant
marked out infants at eight days old, as
embraced within it—did not embrace them
in it at eight days old, but marked or
sealed the fact that they were embraced
in it from birth. Circumcision did not
give children title to membership in the
Church, but sealed the fact that they
were members. And the proof that children were once members of the Church
is proof sufficient that they are still members of it.

Falling back, therefore, on our original
proposition as already demonstrated, that
the Church of God is one and the same in
its essential nature in every age, we are

entitled to affirm that infants once competent members of it, are competent members still. And hence it follows that the
children of parents who have received
baptism—*which is the formal evidence
of membership*—are to be baptized, and
grow up within the pale of the Church, in
New Testament times, as in Old Testament times.

And they who object to infant membership on the ground of propriety and common sense, must settle the quarrel with
God, who originated the charter of the
Church.

And here we must be allowed to express an idea suggested by the quotation
previously given from Dean Alford: Infant membership is THE PATTERN OF ALL
MEMBERSHIP. It is NORMAL CHURCH-
MEMBERSHIP. When we, who are mature, would become members, we must
lay aside all which distinguishes us from

the *little child*—"be converted and become as little children;" and except we become as little children "we cannot enter the kingdom of God."*

"THEIR CHILDREN, ALSO, SHALL BE AS AFORETIME."—Jer. xxx. 20.

---

*For the relation of baptized children to the Church, see close of second chapter.

CHAPTER II.

NEW TESTAMENT ARGUMENT.

IN the first chapter it was shown that it was the practice of the Church under the old dispensation to consider and treat the children of believing parents as being in the same covenant relation to God as their parents, and to submit them to the ordinance which was the formal evidence of this relation.

We now proceed to offer some of the reasons which prove the following proposition:

THAT THE DOCTRINE AND PRACTICE OF THE CHURCH ON THIS SUBJECT ARE THE SAME UNDER THE NEW DISPENSATION AS UNDER THE OLD.

1. There can be no reason assigned why there should be a difference.

Had it not been best for the spiritual welfare of parents and children, God would never have adopted it in the charter of the Church. And if it was for spiritual advantage in one age, there can be no reason why it is not for spiritual advantage in another and in every age. Human nature, human sin, and God's plan for human redemption are always and everywhere the same. What God adopts for spiritual benefit at one time, will always redound to spiritual benefit. If in the divine estimation, it was ever expedient, right and good that children should be admitted into covenant relation with him *in the Church*, and that they should be entitled to the ordinance which testifies and seals their title, which likely none will deny, then we may successfully challenge any party to show why the same things are not always expedient, right and good.

This wholesome principle in the original charter of the Church must be therefore maintained as unchanged, until its abrogation can be proven by an express prohibition, or by an incompatibility, no less distinct, between the nature of the ordinance and their condition as infants. But no such prohibition and no such incompatibility exist, and we are fully warranted in saying that the ancient covenant relation of infants and its necessary consequence, their baptism, still exist.

2. No Jews, in New Testament times, ever made complaint of being deprived of any valued privilege which they had previously enjoyed. There were many Jewish converts and many Jews were added to the Church in the days of Christ and of the apostles. It had been their custom previously to consider and treat their children

as members of the Church, and to administer to them the sealing ordinance accordingly, and if, on their introduction into the Christian Church, they found themselves deprived of these valued privileges, by a radical change in the regulations, we would naturally look for them to lay in their complaints. "It is, therefore, strong corroborative proof of the practice of the early Christians, that while there were multitudes who were converts from the Jewish faith, by whom the admission of their children into the Church by the seal of the covenant, was regarded as a privilege of the greatest importance, and while controversies about circumcision agitated the Church, and awakened the most intense and prejudiced feelings, there is not a single instance recorded, neither in scripture nor history, of any Jewish convert making any complaint or difficulty because deprived of this privilege." The plain presumption is that they were not thus deprived, but that they found the practice of the Church in this particular to be in apostolic times what God had made it for them in prophetic times.

3. The apostle Paul recognizes children as members of the Church in his epistles to the Ephesians and Collossians.

The epistle to the Ephesians begins: "To the *saints* which are at Ephesus, and to the faithful in Christ Jesus." That to the Collossians begins: "To the *saints* and faithful brethren in Christ which are at Collosse." Then the apostle proceeds to address these saints and faithful ones, by the various relations of husbands and wives, masters and servants, parents and children. As: "Children, obey your parents in the Lord."—Eph. vi. 1. And, "Children, obey your parents in all things."—Col. iii. 20. Thus parents, servants and *children* are separately ad-

dressed as being included in the "saints
and faithful in Christ." Now if those
parents were members of the Church, and
the apostle so addressed them, were not
the children also? Note, the apostle here
classifies the *saints* and *faithful* who belong to the Church, and mentions *children* among them, never making any dis-
tinction in their Church relations. He
writes to the members of the Church, and
among them he finds children, and ad-
dresses them as such. By what authority,
then, can any one say that the husbands,
wives, masters, servants and parents,
whom Paul classifies as such, were Church
members, but that the *children* were not?

Respecting the ages of those here addressed by the apostle as children, it is
only necessary to refer to the fact that he
instructs the parents to "bring them up
in the nurture and admonition of the
Lord," showing that they were children

of a very tender age—subjects of discipline and mental instruction. That they were not of sufficient age to be classed as *adults* is also manifest from the fact that they are amonished to obey their parents in all things.

Especially, let the language be noted, "Children, obey your parents *in the Lord*." How could they obey "*in the Lord*," if they themselves *were not in the Lord?* This expression, in every instance, marks incorporation into the Christian body. For example, when St. Paul distinguishes those of the family of Narciscus who were Christians, his language is "which *are in the Lord*." Philemon "was *in the Lord*." A fellow Christian with his master, Onesimus was "*in the Lord*." So also was Amplias, Paul's "*beloved in the Lord*." And so also were the children addressed in the epistles to the Ephesians and Collossians, "*in the Lord.''* The expression means incorporation into the Christian body—Church membership—everywhere else. Will any one say that it does not mean the same when applied to children?

Thus we arrive at the conclusion that St. Paul understood that children were to be regarded and treated as members of the Church.

4. The principle of representation found in the Old Testament, in the case of parent and child, is not cancelled, but continued in the New, *and must be held as a permanent principle.* One passage of scripture announces it: ''For the unbelieving husband is sanctified by the wife, and the unbelieving wife is sanctified by the husband: else were your children unclean; but now are they holy.''—I Cor. vii. 14.

Here it is palpable that the apostle assigns a peculiar privilege to the children

of believers, on the principle of representation, the rule leaning to the side of
mercy in the case where only one parent
is a believer. The child is clean or holy
because the parent is holy: or, in accordance with previous ecclesiastical practice,
the child is entitled to Church membership and the sealing ordinance because the
parent is. This much is certain, that in
the mind of the apostle, the child of a
believer sustains some relation, or is entitled to some privilege which does not
belong to the child of an unbeliever. Let
it be in man's estimation, unreasonable or
reasonable, foolish or wise, *it is true*, and
we cannot gainsay it.

The word *sanctify* means to consecrate
and regard as sacred. Any child, the
circumstances of whose birth secured it a
place within the theocracy or common-
wealth of Israel, was said to be *holy*, according to the constant usage of scrip-

ture. For this reason Paul argues in the eleventh chapter of Romans, that all the children of Abraham were *holy*. The child of a Jewish parent was entitled to circumcision because it was *holy* in an ecclesiastical sense; not in a literal sense; it was a child of the Church. It was not *holy* because it was circumcised, but *circumcised* because it was holy—or consecrated to God and regarded as sacred.

The child of a Jew was treated as a Jew, and Paul seems to take it for granted as universally admitted that the child of a Christian is to be treated as a Christian, and hence does not stop to argue that, but proceeds at once to consider the question as to what is to be done in case only one parent is a Christian—and decides the question on the side of mercy by pronouncing the child, *one* of whose parents is "*believing*," to be *holy*.

The Jewish child when *holy*—regarded

as sacred—was circumcised as a testimony and seal of that fact. The Christian
child when *holy*—regarded as sacred by
virtue of having a believing parent—is
baptized as a testimony and seal of
that fact. It is not *holy* because it is
baptized; but it is baptized because it is
holy.

Thus we are certainly warranted by
scripture in concluding that the principle
on which baptism is to be administered
now is identical with the principle on
which circumcision was administered before—that the principle, on which the
sealing ordinance in the Church has been
administered, has been the same under
both dispensations, and that it has been
applied to infants, one or both of whose
parents have themselves received or do
receive that ordinance.

If the interpretation which we have
here given of the passage of scripture

quoted be not the correct one,. allow us to ask the one who pronounces it incorrect, what the apostle meant by this language? Under any other view than the one we have taken of it, it seems unmeaning. A Jew hearing it would have understood it at once. He knew that the term *"unclean"* meant unfitness for admission to Church privileges, and the term *"holy"* just the opposite. Immediately he would have caught the idea just as we have presented it, as that is in accordance with the previous practice of the Church, with which he was familiar.

5. The total silence of scripture in reference to any change in regard to this principle of representation is, itself, conclusive evidence that no change was made, and of the practice of the early Christians.

The principle of infant membership and baptism being once established as the doctrine of the Church, and its undisturbed practice for many centuries it follows that such is the perpetual doctrine and practice of the Church, as long as the Great Law-Giver is silent as to any change. When any political principle is once incorporated into the constitution of a country, it must remain in force until the constitution is changed by proper authority. Any feature in the statute laws of a State must continue in binding force until repealed by competent power. Silence could never change a constitution nor repeal a statute; but is conclusive evidence of no change.

It is, therefore, not only improbable that God would make an important change in the constitution and statutes of the Church, and say nothing about it, but such is impossible. His silence would be the warrant that no change was made. Therefore, we repeat, the total silence of scripture, in reference to any change on this subject, warrants us in maintaining that what was the constant duty and practice of the Church for many centuries after its organization, is still the duty, and should be the practice of the Church always and everywhere.

It is said that Christ gave no command to baptize infants. We reply that no such command was needed. The command to admit children into the covenant and to administer to them the sealing ordinance, once given, needs not to be repeated, but must be in force, without any additional command.

We may be allowed to remark here that while Christ *made* many changes in the circumstances of the Church, and distinctly announced them, it would be passing strange for Him to make a change in the very charter principles and make no mention of it whatever. Such a supposition is preposterous. Especially so, when it is considered, as shown in Chapter 1, that the apostles understood that the previous practice of the Church in admitting infants was to be continued.

The argument in the last five paragraphs is intended to corroborate historically the principle announced in Chapter 1 that the covenant once made, partakes of the nature of a contract, and even God himself cannot annul it, without doing violence to the immutability of his own promise and to the rights of the creature, the other contracting party.

6. In conformity with this principle of the representation of the child in the faith of the parent, and as evidence that the practice of the Church was to continue unchanged, we mention the following fact:

In every instance of the baptism of adults, recorded in the New Testament, where it is certain that there were children, the children were baptized on the faith of and with the parents.

We have previously shown that the law and uniform practice under the old dispensation were the admittance and circumcision of the children when the parent was admitted and circumcised. And the practice of the apostles, as announced in the above proposition, is conclusive evidence that this law and practice were perpetuated under the new dispensation.

It then becomes necessary to show that there were children in the cases of *household* baptisms mentioned in the New Testament.

This argument alone seems conclusive on this point:

Two Greek words are used in the New Testament which are translated *household*, and have similar, but not the same meaning. These words are *oikia* and *oikos*.

Both these words are frequently translated *a house*, meaning a dwelling. When thus translated they are synonymous in use. But both are also frequently translated *house* or *household*, meaning occupants. When thus translated they are not synonymous. *Oikia* is used when a household of adults is meant, and *oikos* when it is a household including children or infants. An examination of a few scriptures will manifest the correctness of this statement. In the following *oikia* is used:

Mat. x. 24-25: "The disciple is not above *his* master, nor the servant above his lord."

"It is enough for the disciple that he be as his master, and the servant as his lord. If they have called the master of the house Beelzebub, how much more *shall they call* them of his *household?''*

Mat. x. 35-36: ''For I am come to set a man at variance against his father, and the daughter against her mother, and the daughter-in-law against her mother-in-law.''

''And a man's foes *shall be* they of his own *household.''*

Phil. iv. 22: ''All the saints salute you, chiefly they that are of Cesar's *household.''*

John. iv. 53: ''So the father knew that it *was* at the same hour, in the which Jesus said unto him, Thy son liveth: and himself believed, and his whole *house.''*

I. Cor. xvi. 15: ''I beseech you brethren, (ye know the house of Stephanas, that it is the first fruits of Achaia, and *that* they have addicted themselves to the ministry of the saints.)''

Let the reader examine the above quotations, and he will see that in each the *household* is one of adults, as in each the occupants are represented as doing acts of which infants are not capable.

In the following passages *oikos* is used:

Luke xii. 42: "And the Lord said, Who then is that faithful and wise steward, whom *his* lord shall make ruler over his *household*, to give *them their* portion of meat in due season?"

I. Tim. iii. 4: One that ruleth well his own *house*, having his children in subjection with all gravity."

I. Tim. iii. 12: "Let the deacons be the husbands of one wife, ruling their children and their own *houses* well."

If the reader will examine these passages and the contexts he will readily see that children, infants, are included in the *households* mentioned.

"I will, therefore, that the young women marry, bear children, *guide the house*," (oikodespotein,) *despotize the family*,—rule the children according to their own wills,—a guiding or ruling which can refer to no class in a family but *children, infants*, who are to be *despotized*, or ruled, according to the will of the parent.

Both *oikia* and *oikos* are in other places translated *household*, but usually under such circumstances that it cannot be determined certainly whether or not the household was composed of adults exclusively or partly of children. The idea is that where a *household* is mentioned in such a way as to show that adults only constitute it, then *oikia* is used. When it is a *household* including children, infants, then *oikos* is used. This difference in the use of the two words appears clear from the above scriptures, and is uniform.

I here quote a paragraph from Calmet's Dictionary of the Bible, article, "Household :"

"It should be observed, that in the New Testament there are two Greek words which our translators have rendered both *house* and *household*. In their time usage did not separate them. The first (*oikos*) signifies the immediate family of the householder; the other (*oikia*) includes his servants also; and they are not interchanged, in respect to persons in the original. Hence we never read of *oikia* as being baptized, but of *oikos* only; the children followed their parents in this rite; but not the servants their proprietor, master or mistress."

Now in the case of the *household* baptisms in the New Testament is it *household* (*oikia*) as composed of servants, attendants, and courtiers—adults; or is it *household* (*oikos*) as including *children, little ones?* The answer to this question will fully decide the question as to the baptism of infants by the apostles. If *oikia* is the word used, then *children, infants*, were not meant; if *oikos*, then *children, infants*, were meant.

First, then, let us investigate the case recorded in Acts xvi. 14-15: "And a certain woman name Lydia, a seller of purple, of the city of Thyatira, which worshipped God, heard us; whose heart the Lord had opened, that she attended unto the things spoken by Paul. And when *she* was baptized, and *her household*, (*oikos*);" not *oikia*, meaning *servants, attendants*, adults; but *oikos, children, little ones;* "she besought us, saying, If ye have judged *me* to be faithful to the Lord come into *my* house and abide there. And she constrained us."

If any want a clear, indisputable case of the baptism of children, *little ones*, on the faith of the parent, here it is.

Next, take the case of the Phillippian jailor, recorded in Acts xvi. 30: "Sirs, what must I do to be saved?'' Verse 33 : ''And he took them the same hour of the night and washed their stripes and was baptized, he and *all his*''—all his *house*, (*oikos*.) Verse 34, ''And when he had brought them into his *house*, he set meat before them, and rejoiced believing in God with *all his house—panoiki, pas*, all, and *oikos*, household, as composed in part at least of *little ones*.

Also, I. Cor. i. 16 : ''And I baptized also the *household* (*oikon*) of Stephanas.'' And I. Cor. xvi. 15 : ''Ye know the *household* (*oikian*) of Stephanas, that they have addicted themselves to the ministry of the saints.'' Here the apostle, in mentioning the *household* of Stephanas, in one case uses *oikos*, and in the other *oikia*. Now why this difference in the using of these words? Why not use the same word in both cases? The reason will appear at once when the two cases

are considered.. In the latter case he is
speaking of the *household*, or part of the
household, capable of "ministering to the
saints," *adults;* therefore in this case he
uses for *household*, *oikia*, as composed of
servants, attendants, *adults*. In the first
case he is speaking of the *household*, who
were baptized on the faith of the parent,
as in the case of Lydia and the jailer,
and therefore he uses the same word as
used in those cases—*oikos*, *household*,
children, *little ones:* such as were baptized on the faith of the parent, not capable, by reason of tender years, of "ministering to the saints," and hence not
included in the *household oikia*.

Thus it appears as plain as undeniable
facts and good reasons can make it, that
in the households whose baptism is recorded in the New Testament, there were
children, little ones, too young to exercise
personal faith or to minister to saints, or

so young at least that they were baptized on the faith of their parents.

Let us consider these household baptisms further. Again note the text:— "And a certain woman named Lydia, a seller of purple, of the city of Thyatira, which worshipped God, heard us: whose heart the Lord opened, that she attended unto the things spoken by Paul. And when she was baptized and her household, &c." 1st. Who heard the apostle? Lydia. 2nd. Whose heart was opened? Lydia's. 3d. Who *attended* to the things spoken? Lydia. Not one word is said about any other member of her household *hearing*, having the *heart* opened, or *attending* to the things spoken. If any other member of the household was converted it is not mentioned in the record. 4th. Who were baptized? Lydia and her *household*. Now if the baptism of the *household* is a subject worthy of remark

in the record, is it not strange that
the conversion of the *household*, on the
supposition, that they were adults and converted previous to their baptism, is not
also worthy of remark? The sacred historian is exceedingly particular to mention the conversion and baptism of Lydia
and the *baptism* of the household; but
not one word about the *conversion* of the
household. The conclusion is inevitable
that Lydia was the only one converted in
the case, and on her faith the *household*
was baptized. Here is a clear case of
household baptism on the faith of the
parent, and proves that the law of representation of previous dispensations of the
Church was not cancelled, and that the
practice, as it had always previously existed, of requiring adult converts to bring
their children with them into the Church,
was to be continued.

Note again also the text in the case of

the Philippian jailor: "Sirs, what must I do to be saved? And he answered: Believe on the Lord Jesus Christ and thou shalt be saved, and thy house." "And he took them, the same hour of the night, and washed their stripes; and was baptized, he and *all his*." The "*all his*," whether children or not, were certainly baptized. Did they also exercise faith? We propose to prove that they did not; as follows: In the expression, "Believe on the Lord Jesus Christ and thou shalt be saved and thy house," if both the jailer and the persons included in the phrase "*thy house*" were required to exercise faith, then the verb "believe" is plural. If only the jailer was required to exercise faith, the verb is singular. The question is determined then conclusively by determining the number, in grammar, of this verb. Now can it be determined whether or not this verb is singular or

plural?   We say it can without any doubt
whatever; but not in the English, because
in our language the imperative form of
the verb is the same for both singular
and plural.   This, then, is one of those
cases where the original comes to our as-
sistance and settles a dispute, because in
the Greek language the verb has different
forms for the singular and plural imperative.   In the case under consideration the
verb is *pisteuson,* which is the aorist imperative *singular.*   And thus it is demonstrated that the jailer *alone* was required
to exercise faith, and yet on that *individ-
ual faith* the persons included in the
expression "*all his*" were *baptized.*

No man who has any claims to scholar-
ship can deny what is here stated, and
no kind or quantity of equivocation can
escape the force of the fact as it exists in
this case.   *The members of the jailer's*
"HOUSE" *were baptized on* HIS *faith, not*

their own. There is no denying this. The scholar, so called, who will examine the Greek text and deny this proposition would deny Euclid's demonstration of a mathematical theorem.

"The old Syriac version of the New Testament, the date of which is assigned, by Walton and others, to the *first century* of the Christian era, substitutes the word *children* for *oikos*, "household" and "all his," in the passages already referred to; and so, in that very early version, the reading is, "Lydia and her *children*," the jailer "and his *children*," &c. This is at once a correct translation of the original, and a valuable testimony, as to the understanding of these passages in the very region where the apostles labored; and being given while some of them were yet alive, it ought to be conclusive on this subject." —Peters, p. 170.

The editor of Calmet's Dictionary gives

no less than *fifty* examples in proof of the fact, that *oikos*, rendered *household*, when used in application to persons, denotes a family of children including children of all ages, and assures us, that as many as *three hundred* instances have been examined, and have proved perfectly satisfactory.—See *Cal. p. 155.* The conclusions are :

First, That the apostles, who frequently baptized the collection of persons called an *oikos*, but never speak of baptizing an *oikia*, must have baptized infant children.

Second, That *households, oikoi*, as including *children, little ones, ought to be* baptized on the faith of parents. And Christian parents do greatly rebel against God's policy who neglect to thus seal their children in a covenant relation with the Lord.

I have been requested to define the relation of baptized children to the Church.

I begin by quoting Mat. xix. 14: "Jesus said, suffer little children, and forbid them not, to come unto me; for of such is the kingdom of heaven."

The terms "kingdom of heaven" and "of such" need explanation:

1. "The kingdom of heaven" and "the kingdom of God" are synonymous, and are the general name under which the New Testament economy was first heralded by John the Baptist and delineated by Christ. Christian societies arose after Pentecost: and not till then was the term "Church" used. The word "congregation" in the Old Testament means the same as the word "Church," in the New; hence Stephen speaks of the "Church," or congregation, "in the wilderness." The names "kingdom of heaven" and "Church" are both given to the Old Testament economy and are also both given to the New Testament economy; but, as

happily expressed by Dr. Morison, they are not co-extensive in signification and use: "They differ in this respect, that the *kingdom of heaven*, like ALL OTHER KINGDOMS, includes the children of the subjects, while the Church is the society of the subjects themselves." Baptism, therefore, recognizes the infant as belonging to the "kingdom of God," or "of heaven," denoting the general community of God's people as existing on earth. Strictly speaking it does not introduce the infant into the Church, unless the word Church be used in a general sense. It recognizes a relation to or connection with the "kingdom," and to be trained up for Church connection proper.

2. "Of such" does not mean "such-like," which would limit it to child-like adults. To thus limit it is a cruel evasion, to say the least. Considered in connection with our Lord's assurance, "Ex-

cept ye be converted and become as little children ye cannot enter the kingdom of God," it plainly teaches that the "kingdom of heaven" is composed of infants and of infant-like adults.

3. The expression "Theirs is the kingdom of heaven," which is repeated in the sermon on the mount, is identical, the pronoun excepted, in the original Greek with the expression "of such is the kingdom of heaven." There "the poor in spirit," "the persecuted" and others not only composed "the kingdom;" but its honors and privileges belonged to them. And here infants and infant-like spirits compose the "kingdom," and its privileges, so far as applicable, belong equally to infants.

4. I close this part of my argument with the language of Baxter, who so sweetly wrote of, and doubtless now enjoys, "The Saint's Everlasting Rest."

How can infants be 'received in Christ's name,' if they belong not to him and his Church? Nay, doth Christ account it a receiving of himself, and shall I then refuse to receive them or acknowledge them the subjects of his visible kingdom? For my part, seeing Christ hath given me so full a discovery of his will on this point, I will boldly adventure to follow his rule, and would rather answer him upon his own encouragement for *admitting a hundred infants* into his Church, than answer for keeping one out."

As a suitable conclusion for this chapter, I have chosen the following by Dr. Hodge: "The apostles were not settled pastors in the midst of an established Christian community, but itinerant missionaries to an unbelieving world, sent, not to baptize, but to preach the Gospel. (1 Cor. i. 17.) Hence we have in Acts and Epistles the record of only ten separate instances of baptism. In two of these,—viz.: of the Eunuch, and of Paul (Acts viii. 38; ix. 18,)—there were no families to be baptized. In the cases of the three thousand on the Day of Pentecost, the people of Samaria, and the disciples of John at Ephesus, crowds were baptized on the very spot on which they professed to believe. Of the remaining five instances, in the four cases in which the family is mentioned at all, it is expressly said they were baptized,—viz., the households of Lydia of Thyatira, of the jailor of Philippi, of Crispus, and of Stephanas. (Acts xvi. 15, 32, 33; xviii. 8; 1 Cor. i. 16.) In the remaining instance of Cornelius, the record implies that the family was also baptized. Thus the apostles, in every case, without a single recorded exception, baptized believers on the spot; and whenever they had families, they also baptized their households *as such.*"

"FOR THEY ARE THE SEED OF THE BLESSED OF THE LORD, AND THEIR OFFSPRING WITH THEM." Isv. lxv, 23.

CHAPTER III.

TESTIMONY OF THE FATHERS.

IN support of my leading proposition, it is now only necessary to add—That the uniform testimony of the early Christian fathers is that the children of parents, one or both of whom were baptized, were everywhere and always baptized.

1st. Justin Martyr, who wrote about forty years after the death of St. John, says: "We are circumcised by baptism, with Christ's circumcision." Here he makes baptism answerable to circumcision, the very point which we have been arguing, as entitling infants to baptism, on the same principles which entitled them to circumcision.

Again he says: "Many men, and
many women, among us, *sixty* and sev-
enty years old, who were *discipled to
Christ from their childhood*, do continue
uncorrupt." Justin here uses the identical Greek word used by our Savior in
the commission: "Go ye, therefore,
and (teach) *disciple* all nations, *baptizing* them and *teaching* them." To
disciple, according to anti-pedo-baptist
and all other authority, it is necessary to
baptize. Here, then, according to Justin Martyr, were parties who were sev-
enty years old when he wrote, who were
discipled in their childhood, and of course,
baptized in their childhood. This is infant church membership and baptism sev-
enty years previous to the time when Justin wrote, which carries the date back to
thirty-six years after the ascension of
Christ and in the midst of apostolic times:
for these Septuagenarians must have been

young men and maidens, while holy apostles yet walked the earth.

2d. Irenæus was a disciple of Polycarp, who was an associate of St. John, and was chosen by him as the "angel" of the church of Smyrna. Irenæus says of Polycarp, that he remembers and could describe the place where he sat, his features, his manner of life and his discourses to the people concerning the conversations he had had with St. John and others who had seen Christ. This Irenæus, speaking of Christ, says: "For he came to save all persons by himself; all, I mean, who by him are *regenerated* (baptized) unto God—*infants*, and *little ones*, and boys, and youths, and older men." This language, in connection with the circumstances of the author, speaks for itself and needs no comment. It is nearly tantamount to testimony by the apostles themselves.

3d.   Origen, a famous Greek father of
the third century, and the most learned
man of his day, whose family had long
been Christian, and who was born about
80 years after the apostolic age, says:
"For this cause it was that the Church
received *an order from the apostles to give
baptism to infants."*   And, "According
to the usage of the Church, baptism is
given to infants."

The number of Origen's works is put
at six thousand, which of course includes
his brief essays, tracts and letters.   This
fact shows his extensive learning and re-
search.   His baptism in his infancy,
which took place only about twenty-five
years after the death of the apostle John
brings the history of that practice to within the shadow of the apostolic age.

4th.   In A. D. 252, in answer to the
question as to whether baptism, like circumcision, should be restricted to the

eighth day, Cyprian, Bishop of Carthage, backed by a council of sixty-six bishops, stated that there was no need of such delay, for "the mercy and grace of God are to be denied to none that is born."

5th. Pelagius, a British Monk, who lived a little more than three hundred years after the apostles, a very learned man, though a heretic on the doctrine of human depravity, says: "I never heard of any, not even the most impious heretic, who denied baptism to infants."

5th. Augustin was cotemporaneous with Pelagius and was the learned opponent of his heresy. He was one of the most eminent men for learning the Church ever produced and, according to his own showing, had read all the literature of the Church up to his times. He says: "Since they (Pelagians) grant that infants must be baptized, as not being able to resist the authority of the whole Church, *which was doubtless delivered by our Lord and his apostles.''*

6th. St. Austin in the fourth century, says: "If any one do ask for divine authority in this matter (of baptism of infants); though that which the whole Church practices, *and which has not been instituted by councils, but was ever in use,* is very reasonably believed to be no other than a thing delivered by authority of the apostles."

Our Baptist brethren say that the baptism of infants "was instituted by councils." St. Austin, living more than fifteen hundred years nearer the apostolic day than they, says emphatically that it "was not instituted by councils, but was ever in use."

7th. Optatus, Bishop of Milevi, A. D. 360, speaks of baptism in the similitude of "a garment" and proceeds: "Oh! what a garment is this, that is always one and never renewed, that decently fits all ages and all shapes! It is neither too big for infants nor too little for men."

Likewise, it may be remarked, that in these testimonies the Greek and Latin fathers have a single voice, and cover a vast breadth of the Christian world. Origen testifies for the Greeks, Cyprian for the whole of Northern Africa, and others for the wide regions of Asia. Says Neander, the elaborate ecclesiastical historian: "In the Persian church, in the course of the third century, infant baptism was so generally recognized, that the sect-founder Mani thought he could draw an argument from it in favor of one of his peculiar tenets."

Observe that these fathers wrote before the Roman Catholic Church was in existence, and, therefore, they do very greatly err, who say that the baptism of infants is "a relic of Popery."

In conclusion :

Great ecclesiastical, like great political changes, are attended with strife. New opinions and practices are not introduced without opposition. If infant member-ship and baptism are an innovation, when was it introduced, and where was the opposition to its introduction among the early fathers? Such a great change in the doctrine and practice of the Church could scarcely be introduced quietly. It would meet with strong and protracted opposition. But who can show where and when this opposition took place?

The reliable writers of the first centu-ries have transmitted minute accounts of the various innovations and heresies which were from time to time introduced. Ter-tulian gives a list of the innovations of his time, the second century, and Irenaeus, of the same century, wrote a volume of 500 pages, which is yet in existence,

against heresies. Hipolytus, of the third
century, wrote ten books against "*All
Heresies*," in which innovations are carefully catalogued. But strange to say, in
these first centuries the silence of the
grave is maintained as to infant baptism
as an innovation or as to any opposition
to it as a heresy. On the contrary, the
testimony of the writers of these centuries
is unbroken and unequivocal as to its existence and the apostolic authority for it.
"In the first one thousand years of the
church's history there is not a voice raised
against it." Miller.

We may well conclude this part of our
subject by the following somewhat lengthy
quotation from Dr. Wall, perhaps the
most assiduous investigator who has ever
undertaken this subject:

"The sense of all modern learned men
that do read these ancient books, except
those few specified, is, that these books

do give clear proof that infant baptism was customary in the times of those authors, *and from the apostles' times.*" "Lastly, as these evidences are for *the first four hundred years*, in which there appears *only one man* (Turtullian) that advised the delay of infant baptism in some cases, and one (Gregory,) that did perhaps practice such delay in the case of his children, but no society of men so thinking or so practicing, nor *no one man* saying it was unlawful to baptize infants; so, in the next *seven hundred years, there is not so much as one man to be found* that either spoke for or practiced any such delay; but all to the contrary. And when about the year 1130 one sect arose among the Albigenses declaring against the baptizing of infants, as being incapable of salvation, the main body of that people rejected that their opinion; and they of them who held that opinion quickly dwindled away and disappeared, there being no more heard of holding that tenet till the rise of the German anti-pedo-Baptists in 1522."

Thus according to history the first opposition to the practice of the baptism of infants was in the sixteenth century.

We may therefore safely conclude that our general proposition is demonstrated to be the doctrine of scripture and the practice of the Church in all ages—under both dispensations.

"PRO HOC ET ECCLESIA AB APOSTOLIS TRADITIONEM SUSCEPIT ETIAM PARVULIS BAPTISMUM DARE." Origen.

CHAPTER IV.

SOME OTHER ARGUMENTS.

1st. In Chapter first the fact was mentioned that, if the principles there set forth be not correct, Christ must have lived and died without being a member of his own Church. Who can show where and when he became a member unless in his infancy, as had always been the practice of the Church? Certainly none will claim that he became a member at the time of his baptism, for that would present him as setting the example to his followers of living out of the Church until we are thirty years old.

2d. Many have the mistaken idea that we claim that baptism admits the children of believers to the Church. They are not members of the Church because they are baptized; but they are baptized because they are members of the Church in a sense elsewhere explained. By reason of their being the children of believing parents *they are members of the Church* and baptism is given to them, as was circumcision, as a seal of the fact of their membership. It does not admit them to membership, but seals the fact that they are members by virtue of their representation in the faith of the parent. This is exactly the Bible view of the subject, and we shall maintain it as such, whether it appears wise or simple to men.

3d. Every human being born into this world is involved in original sin. Of the race it is written, "There is no soundness in it; but wounds and bruises and putrifying sores.'' But the doctrine in Romans is that the plaster is as broad as the sore. Christ gave himself a ransom for all. Therefore every one born into this world is Christ's until by sin and unbelief he wilfully rejects him. If infants are not Christ's how can they be saved if they die in infancy? If they are his after death, are they not his before death? And if his are they not in some way in a gracious state? And if in a gracious state, are they not entitled to recognition as ''children of the kingdom,'' and to the ordinance which recognizes the relation?

4th. As anti-pedo-Baptists insist on bringing their favorite Greek word *baptizo* into the argument, we wish to give them the benefit of it in the following quotation, 1st Corinthians, chap. x. 1-6:

''Moreover, brethren, I would not that ye should be ignorant, how that all our fathers were under the cloud, and all passed through the sea.

"And were all *baptized* unto Moses in the cloud and in the sea;

"And did all eat the same spiritual meat;

"And did so drink the same spiritual drink; (for they drank of that spiritual Rock that followed them; and that *Rock was Christ;*)

"But with many of them God was not well pleased; for they were overthrown in the wilderness.

"Now these things *were our examples,* to the intent we should not lust after evil things, as they also lusted."

In this scripture the reader will note the following facts:

1. That the *baptizing* in this case, whatever it was in other respects, in its main feature was the same action which is expressed by that Greek word about which

so much is written, as that same word is here used.

2. That all the Israelites—old, middle-aged, young, youthful and infantile—*all* who passed through the Red Sea, "were *baptized*."

3. That the administrator of this baptism was God himself. What, God *baptize* infants! So says the apostle Paul to the Corinthians.

4. That this baptizing, children, infants and all, was done as the apostle says, in verse sixth, "*for our examples.*"

As we are often asked to produce a Bible case of the baptism of infants, we produce this as one which cannot be gainsayed. And let us make an inquiry into this case and see, if we can, how many children there were.

About three months from this *baptizing* the children of Israel were numbered. [See book of Numbers, chap. 1, verse

46.] In eleven of the twelve tribes there were men from twenty years old and up-wards, able to bear arms, *six hundred and three thousand five hundred and fifty.* Double this number for the supposition that the number of women was equal to that of the men, and then add one-eleventh for the other tribe, and you have for the whole number of persons over twenty years old and younger than the age for exemption from bearing arms, one mil-lion three hundred and sixteen thousand eight hundred and thirty-six, (1,316,-836) able-bodied adults. Now estimate how many children are usually with that many able-bodied adults—especially con-sidering the usual fecundity of the Jews —and you will have an idea of the num-ber of children baptized in this case. That there were the usual number of children from *one month* old and upwards, at least, is proven from Numbers iii. 15, where a portion of them were required to be numbered. Nothing is said about children younger than one month, but where there are those above that age it is usual, to say the least, to have a due proportion younger than that, and there is no reason for supposing that they were not here.

To say the least of it, this is a case of the *baptism*, yes, *"baptism,"* of a very large number of *infants*, and God, the administrator in the case. If any deny this, it is a question of veracity between them and the apostle Paul which we will allow the parties concerned to settle without our interference. And if the baptism of infants is foolish and a desecration, God himself is the foolish and guilty party in this case, the apostle Paul being the historian.

Here is a case of the baptism of infants on a large scale. Paul says they *"were all baptized*'' (baptizo), and that it was ''for our examples.'' If any say that this is not an instance of ordinary baptism, then they must repudiate their favorite Greek word, for this is just what comes of giving them the full benefit of its signification. It is a dispute between them and the Greek word.

We must ask the reader's pardon for what follows, as we do not wish to caricature : but we cannot resist the temptation to give just here an illustration of the absurdity to which the immersionists' definition of the word *baptizo* leads. Thus:

Dr. Carson: ''My position is, that it *(baptizo)* always signifies to dip.'' And Alexander Campbell thus defines valid dipping: ''We must dip, only once, and the motion must be backwards.''

Now substitute these definitions for the word in the verse above quoted from the apostle Paul, viz.: ''And were all *bap-*

tized unto Moses in the cloud and in the sea,'' and you have the following rather awkward sentence for so learned and rhetorical a man as Paul, viz.: ''And were all,''—men, women, youths, children and infants—''dipped, once, backwards, unto Moses in the cloud and in the sea.'' And this awkward sentence, forced upon us when we accept the definitions to which immersionists limit us, the penalty being excommunication from all church privileges and blessings, becomes the more remarkable when considered in the light of the following facts:

1. Moses tells us that this baptizing (or ''dipping'') was done on dry ground. Ex. xiv. 29: ''But the children of Israel walked upon *dry land* in the midst of the sea.''

2. David, celebrating the passage of the Red Sea, in sacred song, says:

Psalms lxxvii. 16: "The clouds poured out water."

Then the case stands thus:

Three inspired pensmen testify: The fact: Paul: "They were all baptized unto Moses in the cloud." Where? Moses: "On dry land." How? David: "The clouds *poured out* water."

Immersionists testify: "They were all dipped, once, backwards, unto Moses in the cloud."

We leave the reader to choose for himself between these authorities.

"QUOD UNIVERSA TENET ECCLESIA:" Augustine, A. D. 388.

CHAPTER V.

SOME OBJECTIONS ANSWERED.

1. It is said that the Bible makes personal faith necessary to baptism, and the following quotation is relied on: "He that believeth and is baptized shall be saved." It is argued that the fact that belief is placed before baptism in this text, proves that it must precede it in every case. Let the reader accompany us in a brief analysis of this passage. We will remark first that it is quite evident that water baptism is not meant in this case at all; but for the sake of argument, we will take it that way.

Three subjects are here mentioned, viz.: Faith, baptism and salvation.

We will designate them by numbers. Faith is No. 1, baptism No. 2, and salvation No. 3. Substituting these in the quotation it stands : "He that hath No. 1 and No. 2 shall have No. 3." Now, the position of our opponents is, that the fact that No. 1 precedes No. 2 in the quotation, is positive proof that No. 1 is essential to No. 2. Now let us investigate. If the fact that No. 1 precedes No. 2 is proof that it is essential to No. 2, then the fact that No. 1 and No. 2 both precede No. 3 is proof that No. 1 and No. 2 are both essential to No. 3. This is clear. Now what is the result? Faith precedes baptism in the passage, therefore faith is essential to baptism; both faith and baptism precede salvation, therefore both faith and baptism are indispensable to salvation. Or thus, baptism cannot be without faith, as faith precedes baptism; therefore salvation cannot be without both faith and baptism, as both precede it in the passage. Thus it is seen that the passage proves too much. When an argument proves too much it proves nothing.

The correct view of this subject is what the Bible has so plainly presented, viz: Abraham was circumcised after he believed: his children were circumcised before they believed; and such was the uniform practice of the Church anciently. Likewise, when adults are baptized, it must be after they believe; when infants are baptized, it is before they believe.

2. It is said that faith is required in the case of baptism, and as children are incapable of exercising faith, therefore they must not be baptized. Let us apply this argument to a few passages of scripture, and see how much it proves more than enough. First: "If any will not work, neither shall he eat." Children canno

work, therefore they must not eat. Second: "Except ye repent, ye shall all likewise perish." Children cannot repent, therefore they must all perish. Third: "He that believeth not shall be damned." Children cannot believe, therefore they must be damned. And so on. As in the previous case the argument proves far too much.

3. Again, it is argued that it is foolish to baptize unconscious infants. The argument is that it is folly to administer a sacrament to unconscious infants. It was therefore foolish to administer circumcision to infants. But none deny that this was done by God's direct command. Then God appointed and required what was foolish. This argument proves too much also.

Whence do anti-paedo-Baptists get authority for holding that children are incapable of spiritual blessings in an ecclesiastical ordinance? Certainly not from the Bible; for that precious book tells us that John was filled with the Holy Ghost from his mother's womb, Luke i. 15: and that Christ himself was circumcised when eight days old, Luke ii. 21.

4. It is objected to the baptism of infants that it takes away the child's freedom of choice. When he grows up he may choose another mode of baptism. For the same reason it could be argued that we ought not to train children up to any system of views, lest they might have believed differently if they had received no early instructions. For instance: 1. They must not be trained in the Protestant faith for fear of taking away their freedom of choice. 2. They must not be trained in the Sunday Schools and in the faith of any Church lest their freedom of choice be taken away. If let alone and unbiased by early instructions, they may,

perhaps, when grown up, choose another faith. 3. Any instruction given them in infancy is wrong, because it controls their opinions in future life, and thus takes away their freedom of choice. Thus, also, this argument proves by far too much.

5. As mentioned in chapter 2, it is said that Christ gave no direct command to baptize infants. In addition to what is there said in answer to the objection, we will here say that Christ gave no command to baptize any class as such—neither infant nor adult. He commanded the general duty of baptism, without specifying any class. And if it is objected to the baptism of infants, that Christ gave no direct command to baptize them as a class, on the same ground it must be objected to the baptism of adults; because Christ gave no direct command to baptize them as a class.

I quote from John Guthrie, D.D., of

Scotland: "The demand for a direct command is the more to be resisted that the burden of proof rests on them, not on us: that it is for them to prove the exclusion of infants from the initiatory rite in the Christian church, rather than for us to prove that a privilege which had existed for two thousand years, ever since God had a distinct visible church in the world, was not now to cease and determine."

CHAPTER VI.

THE ARGUMENT CONDENSED.

"To my mind, the argument for infant baptism lies in a nutshell. It is this: The covenant and provisions of God's grace are in all ages the same. The social constitution and wants of man are always essentially the same. The visible church in its vital spiritual features is always and everywhere the same. That the Church began to take shape·in the time of Abraham, and through that entire patriarchal and Mosaic period down to Christ —a period of 2,000 years—it was a recognized and invariable principle that the consecrated community included the children, and shared with them the badge, or initiatory rite. This, and all its spiritual implications, was a settled law in Jacob, and testimony in Israel. It was the state of things when Christ came. At that time, when proselytes were received, their families were received along with them. This is beyond all dispute. The greatest rabbinical scholar, perhaps, which ever England produced—Dr. Lightfoot—says this is as clear as that the sun is shining in the heavens. Proselytes and children were both circumcised and baptized. Circumcision was dropped in the New Testament age, as inapplicable to a world-wide dispensation, and baptism was retained in its place." Dr. Guthrie.

When the Church passed from the old dispensation to the new, Christ made no change as to the relation, privileges and rights of children. The precepts and practice of the apostles, and their silence as to a change, show that there was no change. The uniform practice and unanimous testimony of the Church, unbroken and undisturbed through the long period of the first fifteen hundred years of modern times, testify that the denying of baptism to infants by a very small part of Christendom is a modern innovation.

We here favor the reader with the exposition of the 95th question and answer, of the Shorter Catechism of the Westminster Assembly, by the renowned Matthew Henry:

1. Are Jews and Pagans to be baptized upon their believing? Yes: if thou believest with all thy heart, thou mayest, Acts viii. 37. Will their justifiable profession warrant the administering of baptism to them? Yes: Simon Magus believed also, and was baptized, Acts viii. 13.

2. Are the children of believing parents to be baptized in their infancy? Yes: for a seed shall serve him, it shall be accounted to the Lord for a generation, Ps. 30. Is it possible they may be in covenant with God? Yes: for you have not chosen me, but I have chosen you, John xv. 16. Is it probable they should be in covenant? Yes: for when Israel was a child, then I loved him, Hos. xi. 1. Is it certain they were in covenant? Yes: I will be a God to thee and to thy seed, Gen. xvii. 7. Is it therefore cer-

tain they are in covenant? Yes: for the blessing of Abraham comes upon the Gentiles, Gal. iii. 14. Does the seal of the covenant therefore belong to them? Yes: every man-child among you shall be circumcised, Gen. xvii. 10.

3. Are the children of Christians members of Christ's visible church? Yes: for of such is the kingdom of God, Mark x. 14. Do the promises belong to them? Yes: the promise is to you and to your children, Acts ii. 39. Does the promise of the Spirit belong to them? Yes: I will pour my Spirit upon thy seed, Isa. xliv. 3. Are they capable of receiving it? Yes: John was filled with the Holy Ghost from his mother's womb, Luke i. 15. Are they then to be baptized? Yes: for who can forbid water to them which have received the Holy Ghost as well as we? Acts x. 47.

4. Are the children of believers federally holy? Yes: else were your children unclean, but now are they holy, I Cor. vii. 14. Are they so in their parents' right? Yes: if the root be holy, so are the branches, Rom. xi. 16. Are they disciples? Yes: for the yoke of circumcision was put upon the neck of the disciples, Acts xv. 1, 10· Are they to be received in Christ's name? Yes: whosoever receiveth one such little child in my name, receiveth me, Matt. xviii. 5. Are they born unto God? Yes: thou hast taken thy sons and thy daughters, whom thou hast borne unto me, Ezek. xvi. 20. Are they bound by relation to be his servants? Yes: I am thy servant the son of thine handmaid, Ps. cxvi. 16. Ought they then to be presented

to him? Yes: the first-born of thy sons shalt thou give unto me, Exod. xxii. 29.

5. Do children need to be cleansed from the pollutions of sin? Yes: for they are shapen in iniquity, Ps. li. 5. Is there provision made for their cleansing? Yes: for there is a fountain opened to the house of David, Zech. xiii. 1.

6. Are the nations to be discipled by baptism? Yes: go ye and disciple all nations, baptizing them, Matt. xxviii. 19. Are children a part of the nations? Yes: your little ones stand here this day, to enter into covenant with God, Deut. xxix. 11, 12. And has Christ excepted them? No: suffer little children to come unto me, and forbid them not, Matt. xix. 14. Were the families of believers baptized by the apostles? Yes: Lydia was baptized and her household, Acts xvi. 15. Did Christ himself receive the seal of the covenant in his infancy? Yes: when he was eight days old he was circumcised, Luke ii. 21.

7. Is infant baptism useful for preserving the church? Yes: that our children may not cease from fearing the Lord, Josh. xxii. 25. Was it a great mercy to you that you were baptized? Yes: for we are the children of the covenant, Acts iii. 25.

8. Must we be careful to improve our baptism? Yes: be ye mindful always of his covenant, I. Chron. xvi. 15. Is it a good argument against sin? Yes: how shall we that are dead to sin live any longer therein? Rom. vi. 2. And for holiness? Yes: for we also should walk in new-

ness of life, Rom. vi. 4. Is it a great encouragement to faith? Yes: thou art my God from my mother's belly, Ps. xxii. 10. Is it a good plea in prayer? Yes: save the son of thy handmaid, Ps. lxxxvi. 16. Is it a strong inducement to brotherly love? Yes: for we all are baptized into one body, I. Cor. xii. 13.

"MEN, BRETHREN, AND FATHERS, HEAR YE MY DEFENSE WHICH I MAKE NOW UNTO YOU."—Paul.